My Adventure in Mother Goose Land

This book was written
especially for
Chris Carnal
with love and kisses from
Mom And Dad

written by Alan L. Taylor
designed and illustrated by Paul L. Taylor

Stories and pictures copyrighted © 1974,
by Me-Books™ Publishing Co., a division of
Dart Direct Merchandising Corp.,
4400 Vanowen Street, Burbank, California 91505.
All rights reserved. Printed in U.S.A.
Patent pending.

ISBN-0-915058-25-1

Old Mother Hubbard went to the cupboard,
To get her poor dog a bone;
But when she got there the cupboard was bare,
And so the poor doggie had none.

What would Mother Hubbard do? She asked
Mother Goose to try to find the missing bone.
Mother Goose knew what to do. She flew to
Esch Court in Ann Arbor.
She knew Chris Carnal would help her.

After she told him about the missing bone,
Chris jumped with excitement. "Oh, yes,
I will help you!" he cried. "I would like to
take along Melissa, Scott, and
Derek. We could also take Huck
and a nice kitten to help sniff out the bone."

CITY MAP

ESCH COURT

ANN ARBOR

Mother Goose always travelled on the back of
a large goose. She and her companions nestled
down among the feathers of the strong bird.
The goose flew swiftly into the night sky.
As they sped through the air, a bright star
shone before them. A wishing star!

CHRIS' WISH:

   "Star light, star bright,

    First star I see tonight,

    I wish I may, I wish I might,

    Have the wish I wish tonight."

"I wished very hard to find the bone,"

Chris told everyone.

They soon arrived in Mother Goose Land and
got ready to hunt for the bone. Mother Goose
explained that there were a lot of people
living here who might be able to help them.
She suggested that they start their search by
asking for help from Jack Sprat and his
wife.

Huck and the kitten dashed around,
eager to be on the hunt.

WELCOME TO
MOTHERGOOSE LAND

CHRIS
CARNAL

Jack be nimble, Jack be quick, Jack jump over the candlestick.

On their way through this strange land they
passed by an odd sight. There, beside the
road, was a boy jumping over a candle!

They arrived at Jack Sprat's cottage.

"Mister Sprat," Chris said, "we are hunting for a missing bone from Mother Hubbard's cupboard. Have you seen it?"

"Oh, no, my child," answered Jack. "We have nothing to do with bones."

Jack Sprat could eat no fat,
His wife could eat no lean,
And so, between the two of them,
They licked the platter clean.

Mother Goose then thought they should ask Old King Cole. He might be able to help them.

They came to another cottage and looked in the open door and saw a boy asleep on a bed. They could tell from the look on his face that he was having a happy dream.

Deedle, deedle, dumpling, my son John.
Went to bed with his stockings on—
One shoe off and one shoe on—
Deedle, deedle, dumpling, my son John.

"He is probably dreaming about animals,"
giggled Scott. Little did they
know how right this was! The group left
to continue hunting for the bone.

Hey! diddle, diddle! The cat and the fiddle,
The cow jumped over the moon.
The little dog laughed to see such sport,
And the dish ran away with the spoon.

Later on, as they went along the road, they
saw a black sheep carrying his wool.

"Baa, baa, black sheep,
Have you any wool?"
"Yes sir, yes sir, three bags full:
One for my master,
One for my dame,
And one for the little boy
Who lives down the lane."

"What a funny thing to do!" laughed Melissa,
as they saw a man and a huge pumpkin. "Have you
seen Mother Hubbard's missing bone?" she asked.

"No, no," replied Peter. "I have been kept
very busy right here."

Peter, Peter, pumpkin-eater,
Had a wife and couldn't keep her.
He put her in a pumpkin shell
And there he kept her very well.

CHRIS'
MAGIC PUMPKIN PATCH

The searching party came over a small hill.

They found themselves in a pleasant garden.

"This is Mary, children," said Mother Goose.

"She has the most beautiful garden in the land."

"She loves all the flowers and takes very good care of them," continued Mother Goose.

Mary gave each child a flower as they went on their way.

Mary, Mary, quite contrary,
How does your garden grow?
With silver bells, and cockleshells,
And pretty maids all in a row.

"Oh, what a fabulous place!" exclaimed
Chris and his friends as they arrived
at Old King Cole's beautiful castle.

"Wouldn't it be nice to have these musicians
play at Chris' birthday party on
August 29?" exclaimed Derek.

Chris was led to the throne. He
noticed the king was wearing a Sardonyx, just
like his August birthstone. He politely bowed
to the king and asked: "Can you tell us where
to find Mother Hubbard's missing bone?"

Next Concert

CHRIS'

BIRTHDAY

AUGUST 29

"Ho, ho, ho," laughed the merry king. "I have
been having a grand party here at my castle.
I have not had time to go out around my
kingdom. But if you will look for the shepherd,
Little Boy Blue, I am sure he could help you."

Old King Cole was a merry old soul,
And a merry old soul was he,
He called for his pipe, and he called for his bowl,
And he called for his fiddlers three.

They saw another wonderful sight. A man was selling pies! Mother Goose told the pieman about their search.

"I have not seen such a thing," said the pieman.

Huck barked at the pieman for some pie.

Simple Simon met a pieman
Going to the fair.
Said Simple Simon to the pieman,
"Let me taste your ware."

Special Today

CHRIS'

FAVORITE PIE

A tipped over stool and broken bowl could mean
only one thing: Little Miss Muffet had run
away. She would not be able to help them either.

Little Miss Muffet sat on a tuffet,
Eating her curds and whey.
Along came a spider
Who sat down beside her,
And frightened Miss Muffet away.

They came to another cottage.
They looked inside to see if
someone there could help them.
They saw a mouse scampering
up and down a clock.

The kitten wanted to chase the
mouse, but Melissa
held it tightly.

Hickory, dickory, dock!
The mouse ran up the clock;
The clock struck one,
The mouse ran down,
Hickory, dickory, dock!

HUCK
AND
CATS
DON'T CHASE
THE MOUSE

The road led them beside a small river.
Out in the middle of it they saw
three men floating in a tub.

Rub-a-dub-dub, three men in a tub,
And who do you think they be?
The butcher, the baker, the candlestick maker,
They've all gone off on a spree.

They finally arrived at the meadow Old King Cole had talked about. The shepherd was fast asleep.

"Let's all look around. Be quiet, so we don't wake him up," suggested Chris.

Melissa went one way. Scott went another. Derek went in another direction. Huck looked under the rocks. The nice kitten peered in all the holes.

"I found it!" exclaimed Chris. He had gone around a big haystack. The bone was sticking out of the hay as if waiting for someone to find it. "My wish has come true," Chris told everyone. "Now we can take it to Mother Hubbard for her dog."

KEEP

MICHIGAN

BEAUTIFUL

Little Boy Blue, come blow your horn,
The sheep's in the meadow, the cow's in the corn.
But where is the little boy who looks after the sheep?
He's under the haystack
Fast asleep.

They knocked on the door of Mother Hubbard's
cottage. The nice old lady opened it and
asked them in. She looked very sad as she
told her story to them.

"Surprise!" they all shouted as Chris
showed her the bone they had found.

The old woman was overcome with joy after
hearing of their adventure. "Chris,
you are a hero. Thank you and Melissa,
Scott, and Derek for spending
your time helping me. Mother Goose always
knows who to ask for help."

Everybody was very tired as they flew home on the back of the goose. They were happy they had been able to do such a good job.

Mother Goose was very proud of everybody. She was happy she had asked them to help her.